101 LESSONS TO BE A DAMN GOOD SPEAKER!

DEEPSHIKHA KUMAR

with ANUKRITI BANSAL

PRABHAT PRAKASHAN

ISO 9001: 2015 Publishers

Published by
PRABHAT PRAKASHAN
4/19 Asaf Ali Road,
New Delhi-110 002 (INDIA)
e-mail: prabhatbooks@gmail.com

ISBN 978-93-5322-385-4
101 LESSONS TO BE A DAMN GOOD SPEAKER!
by DEEPSHIKHA KUMAR
with ANUKRITI BANSAL

Edition
2023

Price
₹ 495.00 (Four Hundred Ninety Five Rupees only)

Printed at
Japan Art, Delhi

to our speakers and audiences worldwide

MAY YOU HAVE

excellence in speech, clarity of thought, correctness of interpretation and inspiration of a lifetime

INTRODUCTION

101 Lessons to be a Damn Good Speaker! focuses on new as well as veteran speakers and provides a handy book of never to be forgotten nuances of speech. This book brings to you real-time lessons, learnings, insights and takeaways from India's largest network of speakers and experts - SpeakIn. It is SpeakIn's official guide on being a five-star speaker in front of audiences of any shape and size. The book is segmented into three sections - 1. Content, 2. Delivery, and 3. YOUR Brand as a Speaker.

I am sure this book will open you up to a fascinating world of speech and delivery. Happy SpeakIn!

IF YOU ARE A SPEAKER, YOU DESERVE TO BE THERE.

HAVE FAITH, DO YOUR BEST AND YOU WILL UNDOUBTEDLY MAKE AN IMPACT.

1

CONTENT

"Hey Karen, do you speak?"

"Damn right, I do!"

1.

EVERYONE IS A SPEAKER

THERE IS NOTHING CALLED A PROFESSIONAL SPEAKER, NEITHER IS THERE ANYTHING CALLED A NON-SPEAKER.

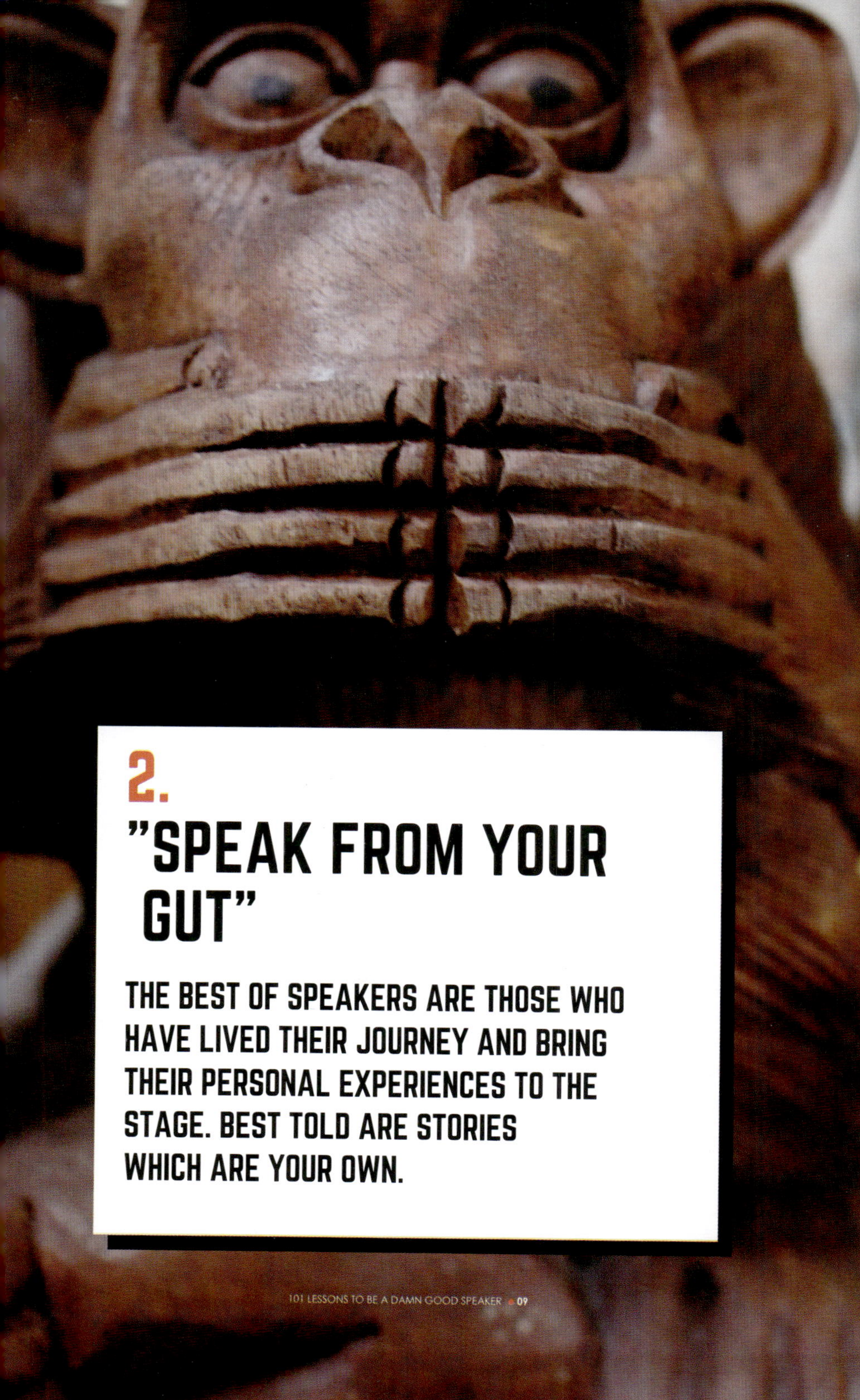

2.

"SPEAK FROM YOUR GUT"

THE BEST OF SPEAKERS ARE THOSE WHO HAVE LIVED THEIR JOURNEY AND BRING THEIR PERSONAL EXPERIENCES TO THE STAGE. BEST TOLD ARE STORIES WHICH ARE YOUR OWN.

3.
FOCUS ON EMOTIONAL ENGAGEMENT

A SPEAKER WHO CAN MAKE HIS AUDIENCE EXPERIENCE HIS CHARACTER'S EMOTIONS THROUGH HIS CONTENT AND PRESENTATION, WINS A SPOT IN AUDIENCE'S MIND. PEOPLE DO NOT REMEMBER WHAT YOU SAID, BUT THEY DO REMEMBER HOW YOU MADE THEM FEEL.

4.

EVERYBODY LOVES A GOOD OL' STORY

STORYTELLING IS AN INTEGRAL PART OF INVOKING THE RIGHT EMOTIONS IN YOUR AUDIENCE. "WHAT YOU'RE TRYING TO DO, WHEN YOU TELL A STORY, IS TO SPEAK ABOUT AN EVENT IN YOUR LIFE THAT MADE YOU FEEL SOME PARTICULAR WAY. AND WHAT YOU'RE TRYING TO DO, WHEN YOU TELL A STORY, IS TO GET THE AUDIENCE TO HAVE THAT SAME FEELING."

5.

ONCE UPON A TIME ______
EVERY DAY ______
ONE DAY ______
BECAUSE OF THAT ______
UNTIL FINALLY ______

EVERY STORY SHOULD HAVE A BEGINNING, A MIDDLE AND AN END, AND A CHARACTER WHO TRANSFORMS FOR THE CLIMAX. PIXAR HAS VERY SUCCESSFULLY USED KENN ADAMS' THE STORY SPINE AS A TOOL TO STRUCTURE THE BEST OF THEIR STORIES.

6.
IF YOU ARE NOT PREPARED TO BE WRONG YOU WILL NEVER BE ORIGINAL

A SPEAKER WHO BOASTS OF REHEARSING, AND EMPHASIZES ON TOO MUCH PREPARATION ISN'T REALLY A SPEAKER. IF YOU HAVE TO PRACTICE TOO MUCH, IT IS NOT YOUR CONTENT.

7.

ISN'T MR. IRRELEVANT THE ABSOLUTE WORST?

APART FROM A STRUCTURE EVERY STORY YOU TELL SHOULD HAVE A CLEAR PURPOSE. WHY IS THIS STORY RELEVANT TO THE THEME OR AT THIS TIME?

"Brilliant copy, it made me cry. It was more moving than Martin Luther King's speech. But Harris, there's one thing I keep asking myself - will it sell dog food?"

8.

SEPARATE FACTS FROM FICTION

DO ENSURE ALL YOUR DATA POINTS, STATEMENTS STATISTICS, EXAMPLES ARE REFERENCE CHECKED WITH CREDIBLE RESEARCH SOURCES. DO ENOUGH PRIMARY AND SECONDARY RESEARCH – ONE INCORRECT DATA POINT CAN ERODE YOUR CREDIBILITY FOR A LONG TIME ON THE SUBJECT.

9.

GO AHEAD AND CHEAT.. ONLY TALK ABOUT THINGS YOU GENUINELY CARE FOR. YOU CAN'T MANUFACTURE PASSION.

10.

THREE IS YOUR NUMBER

BUILD A THREE POINT PRESENTATION. HUMANS ARE BEST WIRED TO REMEMBER AND RETAIN UP -TO THREE THINGS FROM ANY ENCOUNTER. STICK TO THE RULE OF THREE - THREE TAKEAWAYS, THREE DATA-POINTS, THREE HIGHLIGHTS AND MORE.

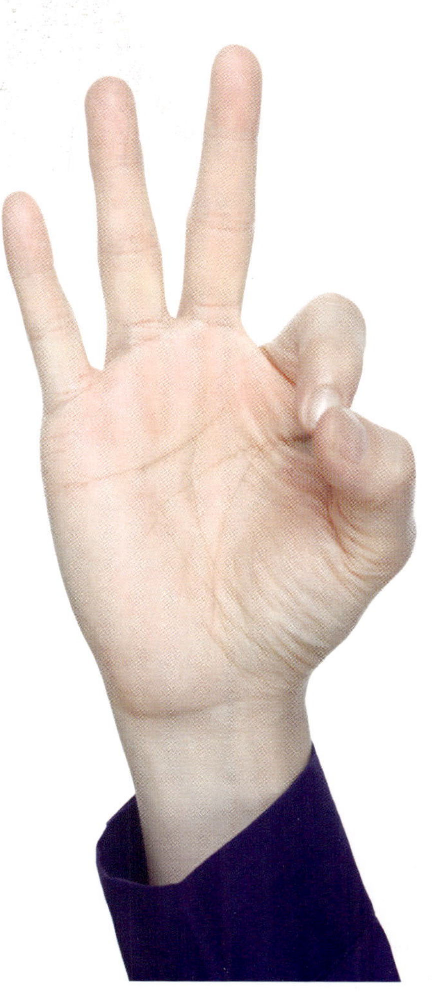

Image Credit - Atos.net

11.

DON'T BE A ROBOT ONSTAGE

DISPLAY OF EMOTIONS IN EXPRESSIONS AND PITCH ARE A CRITICAL PART OF GOOD CONTENT DELIVERY. IT SHOULD HOWEVER BE CONTEXTUAL, IN LINE WITH THE CONTENT BEING SPOKEN ABOUT. IT IS DISTRESSING TO HEAR A SPEAKER TALK ABOUT DEATH AND LOSS OF LIFE WITH A HUGE SMILE ON HIS FACE.

12.

SKIP THE JARGON

EVEN WITH A TECHNICAL PRESENTATION. USE SHORT, SIMPLE SENTENCES WITH EVERYDAY LANGUAGE AND EXAMPLES TO DELIVER THE MOST COMPLICATED OF TOPICS.

13.

STICK TO YOUR MOTIF

UNDERSTANDING OF AND PASSION FOR, A PARTICULAR AREA OF EXPERTISE IS THE FOUNDATION FROM WHERE YOU START BUILDING YOUR SPEAKER PROFILE.

14.

LAUGHTER MAY NOT BE THE BEST MEDICINE,

JOKES ARE A PASSE. ESPECIALLY THE SOCIAL MEDIA ONES. MAKE A LIGHT COMMENT, TELL A STORY, BE INTERACTIVE, ASK A QUESTION, NO JOKES - IT CREATES PRESSURE ON YOU – ESPECIALLY WHEN IT DOESN'T TURN OUT TO*BE AS FUNNY AS ONE INTENDED IT TO BE.
NOT UNLESS YOU ARE A STAND-UP COMEDIAN.

* I have known many a speakers who constantly use social media jokes as punch lines. Such content may have a momentary impact but has limited shelf life.

15.

Know the Event Agenda

Look through the sessions before and after your speech to understand the topics being discussed, other speaker profiles and possible topics which you can add or omit to prevent redundancy.

16. KNOW THE PURPOSE OF YOUR ~~LIFE~~ talk

YOUR TALK, IRRESPECTIVE OF THE TOPIC, SHOULD CONNECT BACK TO THE OVERALL THEME OF THE EVENT, IF THERE IS ONE. IT IS ALSO BENEFICIAL TO DO A PRE-EVENT DEBRIEF WITH THE KEY-STAKEHOLDERS TO UNDERSTAND THEIR EXPECTATIONS AND ALIGN ACCORDINGLY.

17.

AS A SPEAKER, YOUR BEST PRESENTATIONS MUST DO THREE THINGS

17.1

INFORM

HAVE A STRONG STORY BEFORE YOU GO INTO ANY PRESENTATION. THIS SHOULD BE RELEVANT TO THE OVERARCHING THEME, SHOULD BE NOVEL, AND SHOULD RELATE TO THE AUDIENCE (ASK YOURSELF, WHAT'S IN IT FOR THEM?)

17.II

ENTERTAIN

(DANCE, IF YOU MUST)

YOUR INPUTS ARE OF VALUE AND DESERVE ALL THE ATTENTION. TO AVOID MAKING PEOPLE SNOOZE AS YOU PRESENT AND SHARE ADD DRAMA, COLOR, LIGHT HUMOR, AND INTERACTION TO YOUR SPEECH. HAVE A RED BULL, IF YOU MUST BEFORE PRESENTING! EXUDE ENERGY.

17.III

INSPIRE

GREATEST PRESENTERS ARE EXCELLENT AT WEAVING PERSONAL EXPERIENCES IN PRESENTATIONS. SIFT THROUGH YOUR PAST, RECALL STORIES YOU MAY HAVE HEARD WHICH MOVED YOU. SHARE YOUR LESSONS, AND AUDIENCE WILL CONNECT TO YOU INSTANTLY.

18.
GET TO THE POINT- QUICKLY

DON'T TELL THE AUDIENCE THAT YOU ARE NERVOUS OR SCARED OR DRUNK OR HIGH. JUST DO YOUR BEST, MAKING AN EXCUSE WILL NOT LOWER EXPECTATIONS AND WILL INSTEAD SEND THEM ON A THINKING SPREE. EXCEPT WHEN YOU ARE LATE – JUST MAKE A QUICK APOLOGY AND MOVE ON – AUDIENCE WANTS YOU TO GET TO THE POINT.

19. REJUVENATE YOUR NARRATION

I HAVE HEARD SPEAKERS REPEATING THEIR STORIES OVER AND OVER AGAIN OVER SESSIONS AFTER SESSIONS. WELL SOME STORIES WILL NOT CHANGE, BUT A FRESH TREATMENT WITH NEW EXAMPLES OR A REJUVENATED STYLE OF DELIVERY WILL ENSURE YOU STAY RELEVANT AS TIMES PROGRESS.

20.

PLEASING PEOPLE NEVER REALLY PLEASES THEM.. UNLESS YOU HAVE A TAIL AND BARK

SOME PEOPLE WILL NOT LIKE YOU – BOTH FOR WHAT YOU HAVE SAID AND FOR WHAT YOU HAVE NOT SAID. TRYING TO BE A PERPETUAL PEOPLE PLEASER WILL ONLY MAKE YOU BORING AND DRY. HAVE AN OPINION.

21.

HAVE FUN WITH EXTEMPORES

When addressing a topic, remember a three point structure:

1) Introduction to the topic.

2) Body of the topic (this is where you highlight positives and negatives, take a position on one side, present facts and evidences to support your position), and finally, give a

3) Conclusion. This helps you structure your thought process especially during an extempore.

22. CONNECT TO THE KNOWN

USE ANALOGIES AS THE MOST EFFECTIVE WAY TO CONNECT TO AUDIENCES WHEN INTRODUCING A COMPLEX OR A RELATIVELY NEW CONCEPT. THESE ARE USED TO BUILD LIKENESS BETWEEN WHAT AUDIENCES ALREADY KNOW AND WHAT YOU ARE GOING TO TELL THEM – TO MAKE YOUR POINT MORE MEMORABLE ONE. ANALOGIES CAN BE IN THE FORM OF PICTURES, NOUNS, OR OTHER FAMILIAR CONCEPTS.

"It would appear, Hopkins, that your gut feel was only indigestion"

23.

LISTEN TO FEEDBACK. ANALYSE, INTERNALIZE, AND IMPROVISE

PERFECT 10S DO NOT EXIST FOR ANY SPEAKER WHO IS SPEAKING TO AN AUDIENCE OF A SIZE GREATER THAN ONE. HAVING SAID THAT, IT IS IMPORTANT THAT YOU SLICE AND DICE THE FEEDBACK AND IDENTIFY TOP THREE TAKEAWAYS FROM EACH SESSION. AT speakîn WE COLLECT FEEDBACK FOR EVERY SPEAKER FROM THE CLIENT ON A 10 POINT SCALE. THIS IS OUR FOOD WHICH ENERGIZES THE NEXT SESSION.

24.

KEEP YOUR ANECDOTES LIGHT HEARTED

ON STAGE STORIES ARE NOT ABOUT SHARING YOUR DARK SECRETS AND DETAILING OUT EVERY SKELETON IN YOUR CLOSET - BUT A LIGHT COMMENT OR A RECENT PERSONAL EVENT CAN IMMEDIATELY BRING THE AUDIENCE TO YOUR SIDE. LEAVING PEOPLE WITH A SHORT PERSONALISED STORY/ EVENT DOES WONDERS TO THEIR ABILITY TO CONNECT TO YOU.

25.

GET YOUR POINT ACROSS CLEARLY

THE MOST IMPORTANT PART OF WRITING A GREAT, MEMORABLE SPEECH THAT ENGAGES AN AUDIENCE IS TO MAKE SURE YOUR MESSAGE IS SIMPLE, FREE OF JARGON AND STRUCTURED. AS THEY SAY "TELL THEM WHAT YOU'RE GOING TO SAY. SAY IT. AND TELL 'EM WHAT YOU SAID."

"Good evening Tonight's news broadcast will be to the point. Everything's horrible. Good night."

26.

AVOID POWER POINT SLIDES WITH HEAVY TEXT

OFTEN TIMES SPEAKERS USE HEAVY TEXT AND DETAILED NOTES DURING KEYNOTE PRESENTATIONS. IT'S BORING AT BEST AND LAZY AT THE LEAST. DON'T DO THIS. ANY SLIDES YOU USE SHOULD BE AN ENHANCEMENT NOT A REPLACEMENT OF YOUR TALK. IF YOU'RE JUST GOING TO STAND UP THERE AND READ OFF THE SCREEN, WHAT DOES THE AUDIENCE NEED YOU FOR?

27.
BRING VARIETY INTO YOUR CONTENT

SPEAKING IS ONE OF THE MOST SEASONAL PROFESSIONS KNOWN TO MANKIND. BRING VARIETY OF THOUGHT, CONTENT, STYLE AND DELIVERY TO APPEAL TO A WIDER AUDIENCE AND BE TIMELESS.

28.

50 PERCENT OF PEOPLE WILL NOT AGREE WITH 50 PERCENT OF WHAT YOU SAY

AS IN LIFE, ON STAGE TOO 50 PERCENT OF AUDIENCES WILL NOT AGREE WITH 50 PERCENT OF THE THINGS YOU SAY. JUST STICK TO YOUR FACTS, BE OPEN TO LEARNING AND LEAVE SPACE WHERE YOU CAN AGREE TO DISAGREE WITH EITHER THE AUDIENCE OR YOUR FELLOW SPEAKERS. REMEMBER, HUMILITY IS STILL YOUR BEST FRIEND.

2

DELIVERY

29.

"A GREAT POSTURE, HEADS UP LOOK, A CONFIDENT SMILE, A DIRECT GAZE - ALL SOMEBODY NEEDS, WHO IS A SOMEBODY."

- LEIL LOWMDES

30.

"ITS NOT WHAT YOU SAID, IT'S THE WAY YOU SAID IT!"

PRACTICE THE TONE OF DELIVERY. IT'S MOSTLY HOW YOU SAY IT THAT MATTERS MORE.

31.

LOOK ALIVE AND KICKIN'

POSTURE HOLDS A CRITICAL KEY TO ENERGY IN VOICE. DROPPED SHOULDERS, LEANING HEAD OR A HUMPBACK WALK PREVENTS CLEAR AIRFLOW THUS MAKING IT DIFFICULT FOR YOU TO SPEAK CLEARLY. STAND WITH A STRAIGHT BACK WITH THE WHOLE BODY ALIGNED ON ONE AXIS. THIS NOT JUST CLEARS YOUR DIAPHRAGM BUT ALSO MAKES YOU LOOK ALIVE AND KICKIN'.

Image Credit: www.123rf.com

32.

MAKE FRIENDS

/frɛndz/

a person with whom one has a bond of mutual affection, typically one exclusive of sexual or family relations.
"she's a friend of mine"

MAKE FRIENDS WITH THE AUDIENCE. IT'S JUST AN INTERACTION AFTER ALL.

33.

BREAK THE ICE!

USE OF PROPS AND SURPRISES DURING A SPEECH ARE REGARDED AS SOME OF THE MOST EFFECTIVE ICE-BREAKERS IN AN OTHERWISE STRAIGHT TALK.

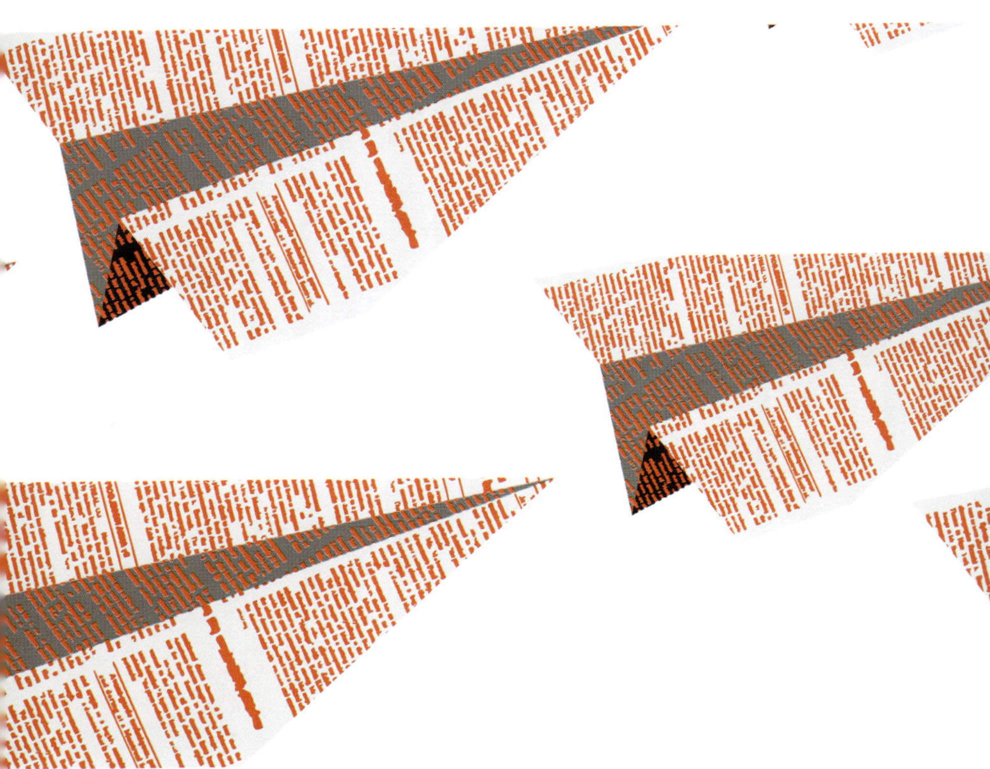

34.

DITCH THAT PIECE OF PAPER

YOU MAKE THE LEAST IMPRESSION WHEN YOU READ OR RECITE, UNLESS YOU ARE AT A CHURCH.
USE ONE-WORD NOTES OR CUE CARDS, IF YOU MUST.

35.

ONE SIZE DOES NOT FIT ALL

CUSTOMIZE YOUR STYLE FOR YOUR AUDIENCE – ACADEMIC, INTERACTIVE OR SPONTANEOUS.

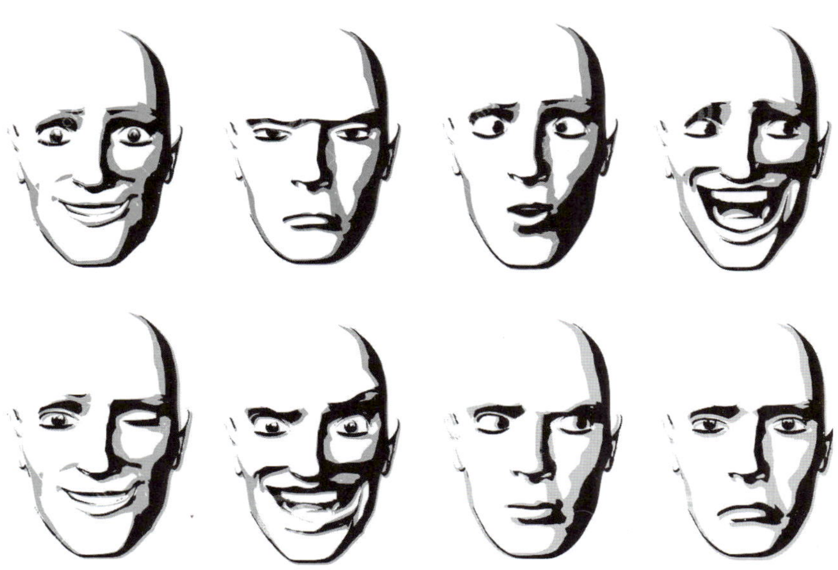

Image Credit: www.dreamstime.com

36.

KNOW YOUR PEOPLE

GETTING TO KNOW YOUR AUDIENCE SIZE, COMPOSITION AND HOMOGENEITY IS ONE PREPARATION YOU SHOULD NOT GET ON THE STAGE WITHOUT.

37.

KNOW SOMEONE WHO KNOWS EVERYONE

LARGER, MULTI-SESSION EVENTS CAN BE PARTICULARLY CHAOTIC. ENSURE THAT YOU ASK FOR A SPEAKER MANAGER SPOC* AT THE HOST SITE FOR ALL YOUR COORDINATION FROM TRAVEL TO BRIEFING TO TECHNOLOGY. SINCE YOUR KEY HOST WILL IN ALL LIKELIHOOD BE SWAMPED DURING THE EVENT, YOU SHOULD KNOW WHOM TO GO TO SHOULD YOU NEED SUPPORT. *SINGLE POINT OF CONTACT

38. INSERT CATCHPHRASES IN YOUR SPEECH

INSERT SOUNDBITES AND CATCHPHRASES THAT THE AUDIENCE CAN WRITE DOWN, RECALL AND SHARE. SINCE MOST OF YOUR AUDIENCE IS ALREADY SHARING YOUR CONTENT ON SOCIAL MEDIA, MAKE IT EASIER AND WRITE THEIR TWEETS FOR THEM.

39.

OPEN YOUR MOUTH, HA HA HA!

OPEN YOUR MOUTH WIDE TO SPEAK AS CLEARLY AS POSSIBLE. WHEN YOU SPEAK WITH A WIDENED MOUTH THE PALATE AT THE BACK OF YOUR THROAT OPENS UP ADDING CONTROL AND DEPTH TO YOUR VOICE.

Image Credit: blog.tillsonlawpc.com

40. LET YOUR BODY DO THE TALKIN'

DURING Q&A ENSURE YOU TURN TOWARDS THE PERSON WHO ASKED THE QUESTION FOR A FACE TO FACE TALK, SUCH THAT YOUR HEAD AND YOUR BODY ARE IN A STRAIGHT LINE. NOT DOING SO GIVES A MESSAGE OF HALF-HEARTEDNESS AND THAT YOU WOULD MOVE AWAY AT THE FIRST AVAILABLE OPPORTUNITY. REMEMBER, ONE MIGHT HAVE ASKED THE QUESTION, THERE ARE TENS WHO ARE WATCHING YOUR RESPONSE.

41.

TRAIN YOURSELF TO SPEAK FROM YOUR GUT

LIE STRAIGHT ON YOUR BACK AND BREATHE. WHEN YOU INHALE, FEEL YOUR STOMACH EXPAND. WHEN YOU EXHALE, FEEL IT CONTRACTING. NEXT INHALE SLOWLY FOR A COUNT OF EIGHT, HOLDING YOUR BREATH FOR FIVE AND THEN EXHALE FOR ANOTHER COUNT OF EIGHT. DO THIS EXERCISE AT LEAST ONCE A DAY TO OPEN THE DIAPHRAGM TO SUPPORT YOUR VOICE AND TRAIN YOURSELF TO SPEAK FROM YOUR GUT.

42.
MAINTAIN EYE CONTACT

ESTABLISH EYE-CONTACT WITH YOUR AUDIENCE (WHEN POSSIBLE). IT BROADCASTS A MESSAGE OF TRUST AND RESPECT. MOST IMPORTANTLY, IT HELPS YOU TO RECORD HOW YOUR LISTENER IS REACTING TO WHAT YOU ARE SAYING AND MANOEUVRE ACCORDINGLY.

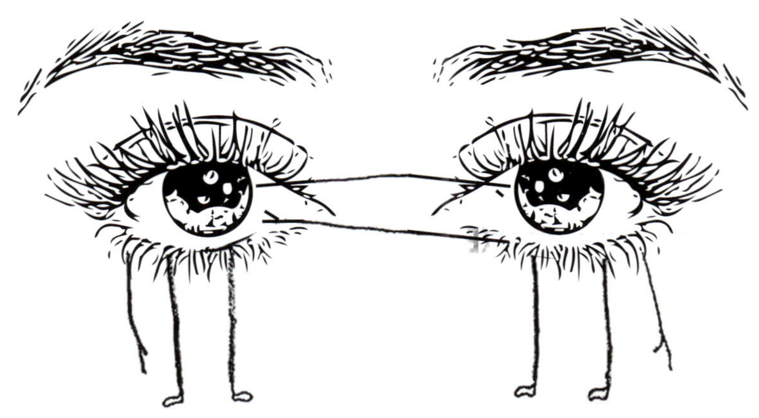

eye contact

43.

CHOSE WHAT FLOATS YOUR BOAT

A SPEAKER CAN DELIVER A MONOLOGUE, INTERACTION, WORKSHOP OR Q&A FORMAT. CHOOSE ONE OR A MIX OF FORMATS PER YOUR COMFORT, COMMAND ON THE TOPIC AND THE AUDIENCE EXPECTATION.

44.

IF YOU ARE SPEAKING AS A PART OF A PANEL DISCUSSION, SEEK TO HAVE A TALK-TIME OF AT LEAST 7 MINUTES

FOR REFERENCE, OPTIMAL SIZE FOR A 45 MINUTE PANEL DISCUSSION WOULD FOLLOW THE 4+1 RULE, FOUR PANELISTS AND ONE MODERATOR. I ALWAYS RECOMMEND LEAVING 10 TO 12 MINUTES FOR POST DISCUSSION Q&A WITH THE AUDIENCE.

45.
"NO, I DON'T HAVE A SHORT ATTENTION SPAN..
OH LOOK, A COOKIE"

THE AVERAGE ADULT ATTENTION SPAN TO A TALK STARTS RECEDING AFTER 15 MINUTES. THANKS TO SOCIAL MEDIA, IT IS NOW GETTING COUNTED IN SINGLE DIGITS. KEEP YOUR KEYNOTE TALKS SHORT AND CRISP. AN AVERAGE CONCEPT BASED TALK SHOULD BE AROUND 18 MINUTES AND CERTAINLY NOT EXCEED 25 MINUTES. SPREAD THE REST INTO AN AUDIENCE INTERACTION AND Q&A WHERE YOU CAN.

46.

DON'T MISS ANY CHANCES TO BE PUNNY!

MORE SEASONED SPEAKERS ALSO USE DISTRACTIONS OR UNEXPECTED EVENTS TO BUILD INTO THEIR TALK. YOU CAN PULL PUN OUT OF A SQUEAKY MIKE OR A PHONE RINGING AS EASILY, WHILE THIS SOUNDS SIMPLE IT DOES TAKE PRACTICE AND COMFORT WITH THE CONTENT.

47.

PRACTICE TO BE AT AN OPTIMAL LEVEL OF VOLUME

PRETEND THAT THE PERSON FARTHEST AWAY FROM YOU IS HARD OF HEARING AND SPEAK LOUD ENOUGH SO THAT HE CAN HEAR YOU. A GOOD COMBINATION OF VOLUME AND GESTURES WILL HELP YOU CONVEY A SENSE OF AUTHORITY AND SUBJECT MATTER EXPERTISE.

48.

INTONATIONS ARE YOUR TOOL TO KEEP AUDIENCE ENGAGED AS YOU SPEAK

USING INTONATIONS VIA VOICE MODULATION HELPS YOUR AUDIENCE TO FOCUS ON KEY WORDS AS YOU EMPHASIZE, DISTINGUISH BETWEEN A QUESTION AND A STATEMENT AND SHOW YOUR EMOTIONS AND TREATMENT OF A SENTENCE. E.G. YOU END YOUR QUESTIONS AT A HIGHER PITCH AND AFFIRM A STATEMENT BY ENDING ON A LOWER PITCH.

49.

READ UP!

HISTORY, POLITICS AND HUMAN PSYCHOLOGY ARE THE BEST READS FOR A SPEAKER – IT TEACHES YOU PERSPECTIVE, MANIPULATION AND HOMOGENEITY OF BEHAVIOR - TOPICS UNIVERSALLY APPLICABLE TO ANY AUDIENCE.

50.

EXPERT SPEAKERS USE FOUR BROAD TYPES OF INTONATIONS FOR A RHYTHMIC SPEECH

*INTONATION MASTERY IS A MUST FOR PROFESSIONAL SPEAKERS. LOOK UP AND DO MORE RESEARCH AND PRACTICE THE FOUR TYPES TO BUILD A VARIED SPEECH.

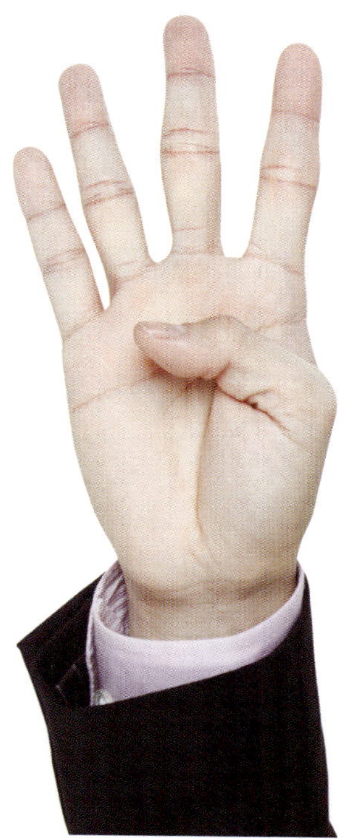

I.
FALLING

WHEN THE PITCH LOWERS AT THE END OF A SENTENCE.

II.
RISING

WHEN YOUR VOICE RISES AT THE END OF A SENTENCE.

III.
RISE - FALL

WHEN THE PITCH RISES AND FALLS WITHIN THE SAME SENTENCE.

IV.
EMPHASIZING

WHEN WE EXPRESS SPECIFIC EMOTIONS OR ATTITUDES WITHIN A SENTENCE BY EMPHASIZING ON PARTICULAR WORDS.

51.

"DON'T YOU KNOW, FINE LADIES DO NOT SPEAK LOUDLY?"

A SPEECH IS USUALLY NOT A CONTEST FOR BEING THE MOST LADY LIKE. WHEN YOU SPEAK TOO SOFTLY, THE MESSAGE CONVEYED IS ONE OF UNCERTAINTY OR LACK OF CONFIDENCE.

52.

LISTEN TO YOURSELF

RECORD YOURSELF AND ASSESS YOUR VOICE AND SPEECH. IS IT MORE NASAL OR FROM THE GUT, FUZZY OR CLEAR, LIFELESS OR ENTHUSIASTIC, TOO SLOW OR TOO FAST?

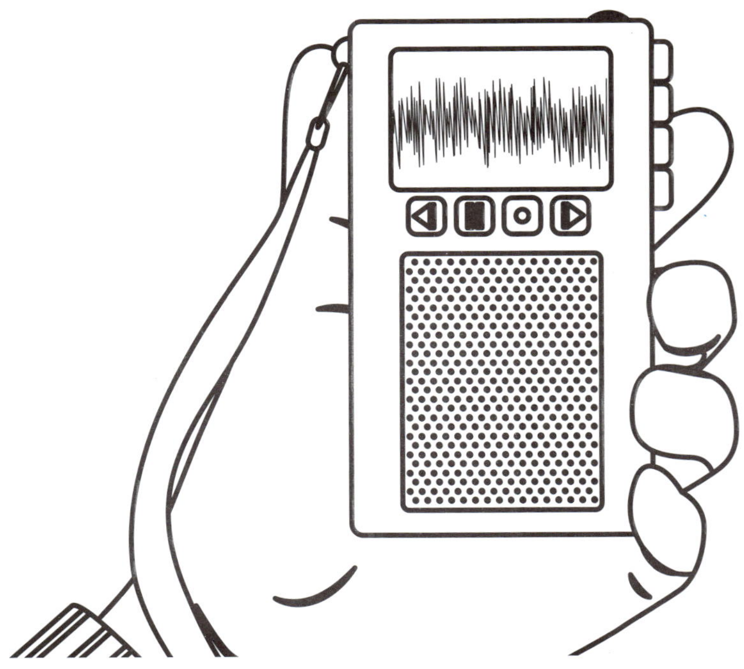

53. BEING ON STAGE IS MORE THAN HOW YOU LOOK

THERE ARE SPEAKERS WHO ARE VISIBLY CONSCIOUS, PERPETUALLY ADJUSTING THEIR TIE/ HAIR. THE PRESENTATION IS NOT ABOUT HOW YOU LOOK – IT'S THAT CONTENT, THE VALUE YOU BRING TO THE TABLE BY VIRTUE OF WHAT YOU HAVE DONE IN THE PAST – AT WORK, IN YOUR LIFE. YOU BEING AT THE DAIS IS A SUMMATION OF WHAT YOU HAVE BEEN TILL DATE. AS LONG AS YOU TAKE CARE OF THE HYGIENE FACTORS – SMART, OCCASION - APPROPRIATE DRESSING AND DEMEANOUR. YOU ARE GOOD TO GO!

54.
SKIP THE MIRROR

OVER PRACTICE, ESPECIALLY THE ONES IN FRONT OF A MIRROR MAKES ONE CONSCIOUS. THE MORE SERIOUSLY YOU WILL LOOK AT YOURSELF, THE MORE CONSCIOUS YOU WILL GET. PRACTICE IN FRONT OF DOGS, WALLS, IN THE BALCONY OR EVEN IN FRONT OF TREES – BUT NOT THE MIRROR.

Image Credit: 10tipsimproveenglishgrammar.weebly.com

55.

FIND YOUR COMFORT ZONE

Looking far up in the vacuum or your feet or adjoining unsuspecting walls can disconnect you from the audience immediately. There will always be people disinterested, sleeping, snoring and even annoying amongst your audience.

Image Credit: www.newyorker.com

"Let me answer your question by saying that you're being really aggressive, and it's totally freaking me out."

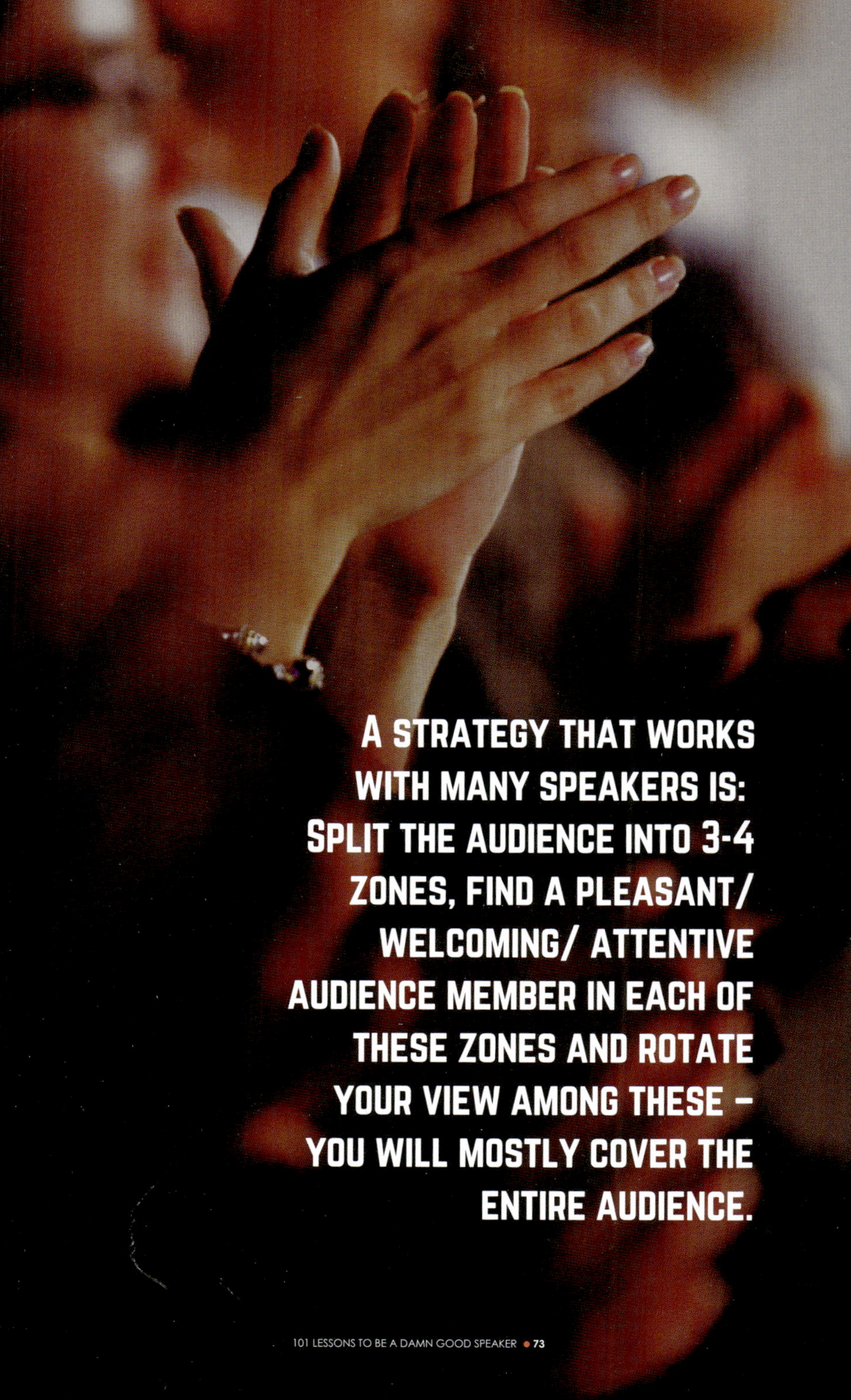

A STRATEGY THAT WORKS WITH MANY SPEAKERS IS: SPLIT THE AUDIENCE INTO 3-4 ZONES, FIND A PLEASANT/ WELCOMING/ ATTENTIVE AUDIENCE MEMBER IN EACH OF THESE ZONES AND ROTATE YOUR VIEW AMONG THESE – YOU WILL MOSTLY COVER THE ENTIRE AUDIENCE.

56.

FIDGETY HANDS ARE THE DEVIL'S TOOL, LITERALLY

KEEP YOUR HANDS OFF YOUR FACE AND OUT OF POCKETS – SCRATCHING NOSE, WOMEN FIDDLING WITH EARRINGS OR FINGER-RINGS – NO.
HANDS SHOULD BE AWAY FROM YOUR BODY AND SHOULD BE USED TO FURTHER YOUR THOUGHTS AND EXPRESS YOUR WORDS BETTER. ANYWHERE ELSE, THEY SIGNIFY LACK OF CONFIDENCE.

Image Credit: www.timeout.com

57.

CAPITALIZE ON DISTRACTIONS

DISTRACTIONS ARE MOMENTS WHEN YOU CAN SHOW YOUR CALMEST SELF ON STAGE. NEVER DRAG A MOMENT OF DISTRACTION - A SQUEAKY MIKE, A POWER-FAILURE, OR MOBILE RINGING, MOVE ON WITH YOUR PRESENTATION AS SOON AS YOU CAN. TAKE A SMALL PAUSE (FRACTION OF A SECOND) IF YOU MAY TO ENSURE ITS NOT A SAFETY BREACH, BUT MOVE ON AS QUICKLY AS POSSIBLE.

Image Credit: vox.xom

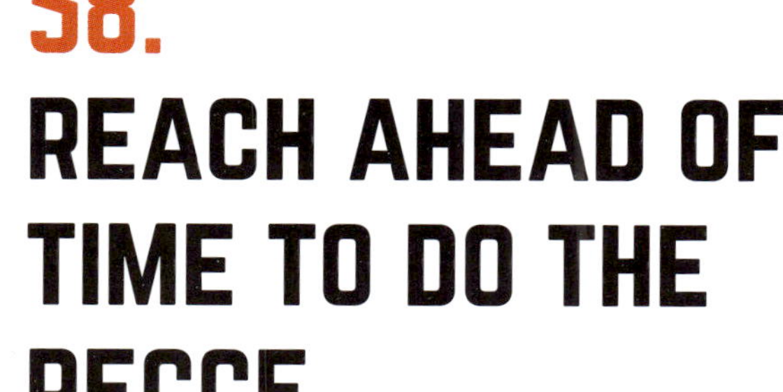

58. REACH AHEAD OF TIME TO DO THE RECCE

GET ACQUAINTED WITH THE VENUE, STAGE AND TECHNOLOGY THAT WILL BE USED DURING YOUR SESSION. REACH AHEAD OF TIME TO DO THE RECCE. THIS IS JUST ONE OF THE THINGS WHERE A GOOD ONSITE MANAGER OR A SPEAKER MANAGEMENT FIRM CAN HELP IF YOU ARE ALLIED TO ONE.

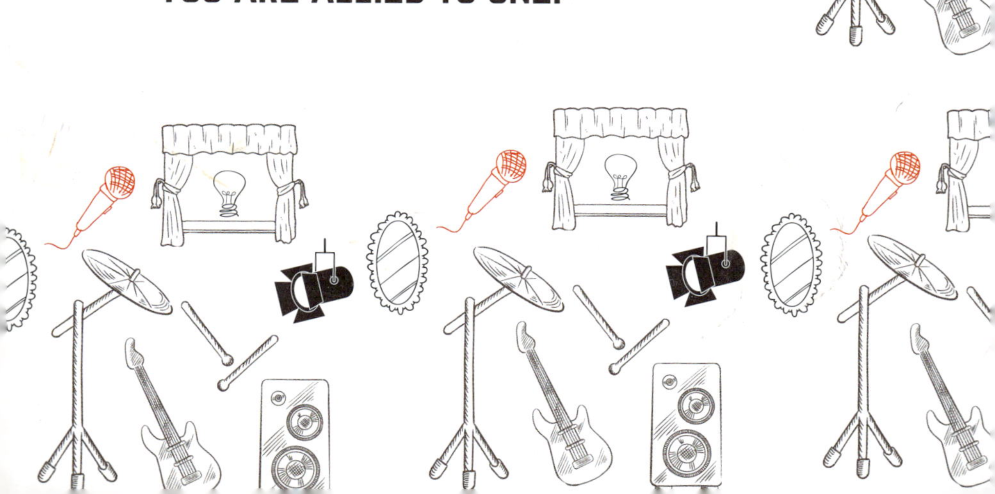

59.
CHECK ALL THE TECHNICAL ASPECTS BEFOREHAND

MANY SPEAKERS ARE CONCERNED WITH THE CONFIDENTIALITY OF THE CONTENT THEY ARE PRESENTING AND THUS PREFER TO USE THEIR OWN LAPTOPS TO PROJECT. THIS CAN BE SUPER TRICKY AND EMBARRASSING IF YOU HAVE NOT DONE A PRE-CHECK ON THE COMPATIBILITY OF YOUR EQUIPMENT WITH EVENT SYSTEMS. DO YOU HAVE THE RIGHT CONNECTOR? DO YOU NEED INTERNET? IS THE SOUND WORKING?

60.

STUTTERING SCREAMS BAD SPEECH

BUILD CLARITY OF SPEECH THROUGH TONGUE TWISTERS. THESE NOT ONLY HELP IN CLEARING PRONUNCIATION BUT ALSO HELP IN EXERCISING THE FACIAL MUSCLES WHICH CAN BENEFIT EXPRESSIONS AND KEEPING A LUCID TONE IN TIMES OF STAGE STRESS.

Image Credit: http://www.famous-ships.info

61.

WATER IS YOUR BEST FRIEND

KEEP YOUR VOCAL CHORDS HYDRATED ESPECIALLY DURING LONG TALKING SESSIONS. STILL-WATER WILL KEEP YOU GOING, WHILE AERATED DRINKS, ALCOHOL AND COFFEE CAN DEHYDRATE YOU.

Image Credit: www.chemistryworld.com

3

YOUR BRAND

62.

DO NOT COMPROMISE ON YOUR ONLY PRODUCT – YOU!

HOWSOEVER FANCY IT SEEMS, BEING AT THE CENTER OF ATTENTION TAKES A LOT OUT OF A PERSON. ADRENALINE SURGE, EARLY MORNINGS, LATE NIGHTS, CONSTANT FEEDBACK AND PRESSURE TO DELIVER EACH TIME YOU GET ON THE STAGE IS ENOUGH TO ERODE YOUR WELL-BEING EVEN BEFORE YOU REACH YOUR PEAK. HYDRATION, DIET, EXERCISE AND OPTIMAL SLEEP WILL ENSURE YOU ARE ENERGIZED ENOUGH TO CONTINUE LEARN AND SHARE FOR AS LONG AS YOU LIKE.

63.

SOMETIMES, QUANTITY > QUALITY

FOR STARTERS, BUILDING YOUR PROFILE IS A PURE VOLUME PLAY. SPEAK IN AS MANY FORUMS AS POSSIBLE, MONEY – FAME – PR WILL COME. ONLY TICK-MARK WHEN SAYING YES TO AN INVITATION IS THE RELEVANCE OF TOPIC – ENSURE THAT THE THEME AND AUDIENCE EXPECTATION IS IN LINE WITH YOUR EXPERTISE AND THEN GO AHEAD AND CHARM THEM!

64.

DON'T BE SHY OF SHARING WHAT DRIVES YOU

WHENEVER I HAVE BUMPED INTO A GREAT SPEAKER, I HAVE HEARD A STORY - A PERSONAL ONE, FAMILIAL ONE OR SOMETHING THAT IS IMPORTANT TO HER IN A NON-PROFESSIONAL WAY. IT INSTANTLY MAKES THE OTHER PERSON FEEL LIKE BEING A PART OF SOMETHING CLOSER.

- Martin Luther King

65.

HUMILITY IS ALL YOU NEED TO BE TOOLED WITH WHEN YOU GET ON STAGE

THE ADRENALINE RUSH AND THE PERCEPTION OF POWER WHEN ELEVATED ONTO A STAGE IS NORMAL. A SPEAKER WHO WALKS AWAY WITH AN AUDIENCE CONNECT IS VALUED MUCH HIGHER THAN THE ONE WHO WALKS OUT WITH A SUPERIORITY COMPLEX.

66. SHOW ME THE MONEY, HONEY

MOST OF THE SPEAKERS COMING TO speakîn TELL ME THEY ARE UNCOMFORTABLE ASKING FOR MONEY TO SPEAK - EVEN THOUGH IT INVOLVES EXTENSIVE PREPARATION AND EFFORT ON THE SPEAKER'S PART TO MAKE THAT SPEECH.

WHILE HOW MUCH TO ASK FOR IS A TOPIC TOO DETAILED FOR SCOPE OF THIS BOOK, IF YOU ARE LOOKING AT MONETIZING THE SPEECH IT IS ALWAYS A GOOD IDEA TO BRING IT UP THE FIRST TIME YOU RECEIVE THE INVITE. "DELIGHTED TO HEAR ABOUT YOUR EVENT, SOUNDS LIKE EXCITING CONTENT. COULD YOU SHARE SOME MORE DETAILS ON THE AUDIENCE - SIZE AND SENIORITY, KEY STAKEHOLDERS, AND THE BUDGET FOR THE SPEAKER?" THIS SHOULD BE ENOUGH TO GET A CONVERSATION STARTED. ALTERNATIVELY GUIDE THE HOSTS TO YOUR SPEAKER MANAGEMENT COMPANY TO MANAGE THIS FOR YOU. THERE IS NOTHING WRONG WITH ASKING TO BE COMPENSATED FOR YOUR VALUE, TIME AND CONTENT.

HAVING SAID
THAT ...

67.
YOU ARE HUMAN, NOT A COMMODITY

PRICE YOURSELF WITH THE OPPORTUNITY COST IN VIEW. THERE IS NOTHING CALLED AN MRP FOR YOUR PRESENCE. EACH EVENT BRINGS A UNIQUE VALUE TO YOU IN TERMS OF NETWORKING, EXPERIENCE, LEARNING AND BRANDING - EVALUATE EACH OPPORTUNITY ACCORDINGLY.

Image credit : dylanwoodlouse.wordpress.com

68.
GROW YOURSELF. NOT JUST YOUR POCKETS

LIKE IN ANY OTHER SPHERE, THERE IS NO SUBSTITUTE FOR EXPERIENCE IN PUBLIC SPEAKING. AS A SPEAKER, ALWAYS CHOOSE A NEW EXPERIENCE OVER MONEY.

69.
HAVE AN OPINION

HAVE AN OPINION AND SPEAK ABOUT THE ISSUES YOU FEEL STRONGLY ABOUT IN YOUR AREA OF EXPERTISE. THIS KEEPS YOU RELEVANT AND IN-THE-PUBLIC-EYE AND HELPS YOU ATTRACT THE RIGHT PEOPLE IN YOUR GENRE. BESIDES, IT IS ALWAYS EASY TO BE OPINIONATED WHEN YOU ARE PASSIONATE ABOUT SOMETHING.

70. Treat your audience well and they will make you a superstar

It surprises me when I meet speakers who want to restrict photography or recording during their sessions. Unless it is a controversial, media-barred session, 3rd party sharing is free marketing for you. Don't worry about being copied – you should be your own competition.

71.
TAG ORGANISERS AND THEIR LIGHT-MAN

SOCIAL MEDIA AMPLIFICATION IS THE CHEAPEST AND QUICKEST WAY TO PROMOTE YOURSELF TODAY - AND IS ALSO HYGIENE. USE EVENT FLYERS PRE-EVENT TO SHARE ON SOCIAL MEDIA CHANNELS. SIMILARLY AT THE EVENT, REQUEST SOMEONE TO CLICK A FEW PICTURES OF YOU SPEAKING ON THE DIAS, PREFERABLY A BACK SHOT WHERE AUDIENCE IS VISIBLE TOO. YOU CAN ALSO SEND A SELF RECORDED VIDEO "I AM LOOKING FORWARD TO SEE YOU AT XXX ON XXX, CATCH ME LIVE." I ASSURE YOU, HOSTS WOULD LOVE THIS INITIATIVE.

POST-EVENT, REMEMBER TO POST AND TAG (THE HOST AND FELLOW SPEAKERS) IN THE PICTURES YOU TOOK. ENCOURAGE ORGANIZERS TO LIKE, SHARE AND RETWEET THE POST, YOU SHOULD DO THE SAME FOR THEIR POSTS.

72.

who run the world?
APPEARANCES

IN THE SOCIAL REALM, APPEARANCES ARE THE BAROMETER OF ALMOST ALL OF OUR JUDGMENTS, AND YOU MUST NEVER BE MISLED INTO BELIEVING OTHERWISE. ONE FALSE SLIP, ONE AWKWARD OR SUDDEN CHANGE IN YOUR APPEARANCE, CAN PROVE DISASTROUS. KNOW WHAT YOU STAND FOR AND THEN STICK TO IT.

73.

MARKET YOUR INDIVIDUALITY

IN THE BEGINNING, YOU MUST WORK TO ESTABLISH A REPUTATION FOR ONE OUTSTANDING QUALITY, WHETHER CONTENT OR A PARTICULAR STYLE OF DELIVERY. THIS QUALITY SETS YOU APART AND GETS OTHER PEOPLE TO TALK ABOUT YOU. YOU THEN MAKE YOUR REPUTATION KNOWN TO AS MANY PEOPLE AS POSSIBLE, AND WATCH AS IT SPREADS LIKE WILDFIRE.

74.
So Much Depends on Your Reputation, Guard It with Your Life

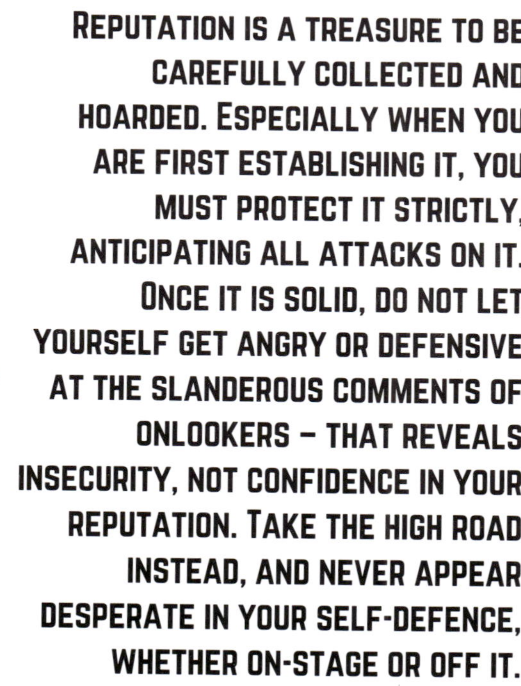

Reputation is a treasure to be carefully collected and hoarded. Especially when you are first establishing it, you must protect it strictly, anticipating all attacks on it. Once it is solid, do not let yourself get angry or defensive at the slanderous comments of onlookers – that reveals insecurity, not confidence in your reputation. Take the high road instead, and never appear desperate in your self-defence, whether on-stage or off it.

75.

BE THE MASTER OF YOUR FATE, AND ALSO OF YOUR REPUTATION

SINCE WE MUST LIVE IN SOCIETY AND MUST DEPEND ON THE OPINIONS OF OTHERS, THERE IS NOTHING TO BE GAINED BY NEGLECTING YOUR REPUTATION. BY NOT CARING HOW YOU ARE PERCEIVED, YOU LET OTHERS DECIDE THIS FOR YOU.

76. LISTEN UP BUDDY!

THE BEST LISTENERS MAKE THE BEST SPEAKERS. IT MAY SOUND CONTRARY BUT LISTENING IS THE MOST UNDERSTATED QUALITY OF A GOOD SPEAKER - LISTEN TO YOUR AUDIENCE, LEARN TO INTERACT, ENCOURAGE NEW VIEWS, THOUGHTS AND EXPRESSIONS. THESE ARE NOT JUST GOOD FOR PERSONAL COMMUNICATION BUT CAN ALSO BE EXCELLENT FOOD FOR YOUR NEXT TALK.

REMEMBER - ON-STAGE SPEAKING AND OFF-STAGE CONTINUOUS LEARNING.

77.

PERFECTION IS OVERRATED

GREAT SPEAKERS ARE NOT PERFECT, TO TELL YOU THE TRUTH, SOME ARE DEEPLY FLAWED HUMAN BEINGS. SO DON'T WAIT FOR A PERFECT MOMENT TO GET ONTO THE STAGE - THERE NEVER WILL BE ONE.

Image credit http://chadayarampat.blogspot.com

78.

DRESS FOR THE OCCASION

YOUR LOOK ON THE STAGE SHOULD RESONATE WITH YOUR TOPIC, AUDIENCE AND YOUR REPUTATION – BUSINESS, HUMOUR, SPIRITUAL OR SOMETHING ELSE.

79.

PHYSICALLY PRESENT.. DIGITALLY ~~ABSENT~~ popular

START BUILDING YOUR REPUTATION BEFORE YOU START YOUR SPEAKER JOURNEY THROUGH ARTICLES, PUBLISHED BLOGS, VIDEOS, IN THAT ORDER. THIS WILL BE THE PRECURSOR TO ESTABLISH YOUR BRAND AS A SPEAKER. FOR EXAMPLE AT speakîn WE USE AN ELABORATE SEMP MODEL TO HELP SPEAKERS BUILD A DIGITAL PROFILE WHICH THEY CAN USE TO SHARE WITH POTENTIAL CLIENTS AND AUDIENCES.

80. DON'T OVERTHINK OR OVERDO

CRISP AND COMFORTABLE ARE THE ONLY TWO RULES WHEN CHOOSING A STAGE ATTIRE.

81.

GENIALITY IS A TWO WAY STREET

ASSUMING NEUTRAL CONTENT, A PRESENTER'S LIKABILITY IS CRITICAL TO HOW WELL HIS/HER MESSAGE IS RECEIVED. AND LIKABILITY IS ALWAYS A TWO WAY STREET. FOR YOUR AUDIENCE TO LIKE YOU, YOU HAVE TO LIKE THEM FIRST, AND SHOW IT AS YOU INTERACT BEFORE, DURING AND AFTER THE PRESENTATION.

Image credit - drexel.edu

82.

GET RID OF YOUR GOD COMPLEX

I HAVE SEEN THE BEST OF PRESENTATIONS SUFFER JUST BECAUSE THE PRESENTER OOZED SUPERIORITY - TOTALLY UNNECESSARY, ISN'T IT? THE FACT THAT YOU ARE THE ONE STANDING AND TALKING IS PROOF ENOUGH THAT YOU ARE IN A HIGHER CHAIR AT THAT POINT. AUDIENCE'S UNCONSCIOUS PERCEPTION IS CRITICAL IN A DECIDER PRESENTATION, SHAPE IT WITH YOUR SMILE.

image credit: DJBooth.net

83.

SUCCESS IS STAYING TRUE TO YOUR ROOTS

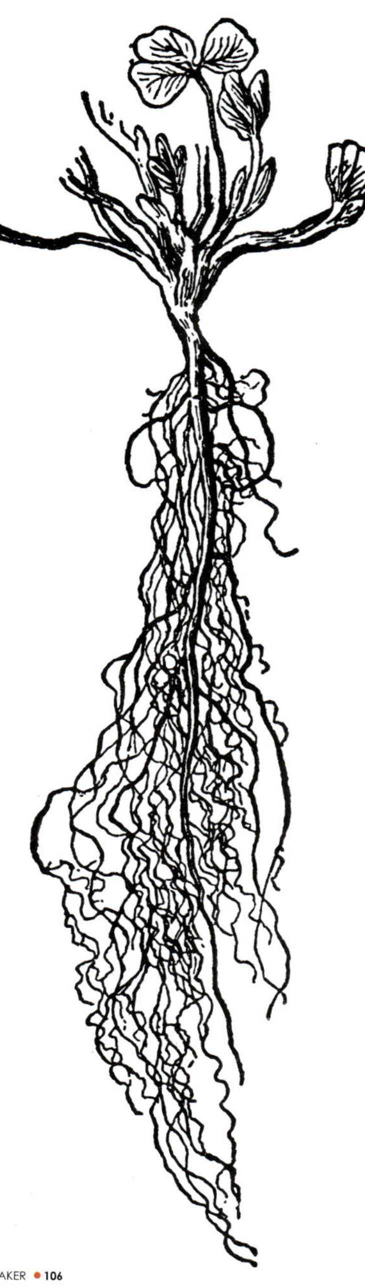

BE TRUE TO YOUR ORIGINS. NOTHING IS A BIGGER PUT-OFF THAN A SPEAKER WHO DISCONNECTS FROM HIS ORIGINAL IDENTITY. STAGE IS FOR ACTORS, NOT FOR SPEAKERS WITH CONTENT. ITS NOT REEL TIME, ITS REAL-TIME FOR YOU.

84.

TAKE PRIDE IN WHO YOU ARE FOR THE AUDIENCE TO RESPECT AND RECOGNIZE

WHEN ON STAGE, BE TRUE TO YOUR COUNTRY, RELIGION, CASTE, OR CREED. THEY SHAPE YOUR ORIGIN WHICH SHAPES YOUR MIND, ANCHORS YOUR IDENTITY, INFLUENCES YOUR BELIEFS, AND MAKES YOU WHO YOU ARE.

85.

REMEMBER TO MEASURE YOUR SUCCESS

YOU CAN USE MULTIPLE WAYS TO DO THIS - FOR THE HOST, AND THOSE IN THE AUDIENCE YOU HAVE THE CONTACT FORM, A SIMPLE GOOGLE FEEDBACK FORM WOULD BE JUST ENOUGH (YOU CAN FIND MANY AUDIENCE FEEDBACK FORMS ONLINE, ELSE JUST LOGIN TO WWW.SPEAKIN.CO/RESOURCES TO FIND ONE).

ALTERNATIVELY, IF THE EVENT HOSTS ALLOW OR IF ITS YOUR OWN EVENT, A SINGLE-PAGER PRINTED FEEDBACK FORM IS A GREAT TOOL TO GET INSTANT REVIEW.

86.

IT'S A PRO-SPEAKING ECOSYSTEM, DIGITAL WORLD BACKED BY INNUMERABLE NUMBER OF EVENTS GLOBALLY ARE SCOUTING FOR GOOD SPEAKERS 24/7 – BUT NONE OF THIS WILL AIDE WHILE YOU SIT BACK. YOU WILL HAVE TO REACH OUT. ASK ANY SUCCESSFUL SPEAKER, HOW THEY GOT TO WHERE THEY ARE, AND CHANCES ARE THEY HAD SOMEONE - OR SEVERAL SOMEONES - HELPING THEM ALONG THE WAY - MEET AS MANY PEOPLE AS YOU CAN, LEARN THE LANGUAGE OF YOUR TOPIC, GET EXPERTS TO CRITIQUE YOUR STYLE AND CONTENT. THE MORE RELATIONSHIPS YOU HAVE, THE MORE ACCESS YOU HAVE TO INFORMATION AND RESOURCES. FOR STARTERS, THERE IS WWW.SPEAKIN.CO.

87.

SPEAKING IS NOT A PUSH BUT A PULL PROFESSION

PUSHING YOUR WAY INTO AN EVENT IS A CARDINAL SIN FOR A SPEAKER. THAT'S WHERE YOU NEED CREDIBLE PARTNERS AND MARKETEERS TO MARKET YOUR BRAND AS A CONTENT AND DELIVERY EXPERT. ESTABLISHED NETWORKS LIKE speakîn HAVE HELPED THOUSANDS OF SPEAKERS FIND THEIR NICHE AND RELEVANT AUDIENCE WORLD OVER. USE THESE TO MAKE A START.

88.
CREATE A SPEAKERS RESUME

KEEP A SHORT AND LONG BIO HANDY TO BE ABLE TO SEND IT TO CONFERENCE ORGANIZERS FOR YOUR SPEAKER PROFILE. TAKE TIME TO CUSTOMIZE IT EACH TIME ACCORDING TO THAT EVENT. YOU WANT TO BE RELEVANT TO THE READERS.

89.

INTRODUCE YOURSELF TO THE AUDIENCE ROYALLY

DO NOT UNDERESTIMATE THE IMPORTANCE OF A STRONG INTRODUCTION. TAKE TIME BEFORE THE EVENT WITH THE HOST TO DEVELOP A SHORT (50-WORDS) AND LONG (150-WORDS) BIO OF YOURS. REHEARSE WITH THE EMCEE TO ENSURE HE/SHE PLACES THE NOUNS AND THEIR PRONUNCIATIONS CLEARLY.

90.

FIRST IMPRESSIONS MATTER

INVEST IN A GOOD PICTURE. A PROFESSIONAL HEAD SHOT AND A CANDID WAIST HEIGHT SHOT CAN SPEAK LOUDLY FOR YOU EVEN BEFORE YOU GET ON THE STAGE.

91.

IT'S NOT JUST YOU!

TO AN AUDIENCE, AN EVENT IS A SUCCESS IF THREE THINGS HOLD WELL:

1. CONTENT: WHAT DID THEY LEARN?
2. NETWORK: WHOM DID THEY MEET?
3. VENUE: WAS IT CONVENIENT.

IF THE ABOVE ARE IN ORDER, YOU WILL MOSTLY LEAVE YOUR AUDIENCE WITH A POSITIVE IMPRESSION.

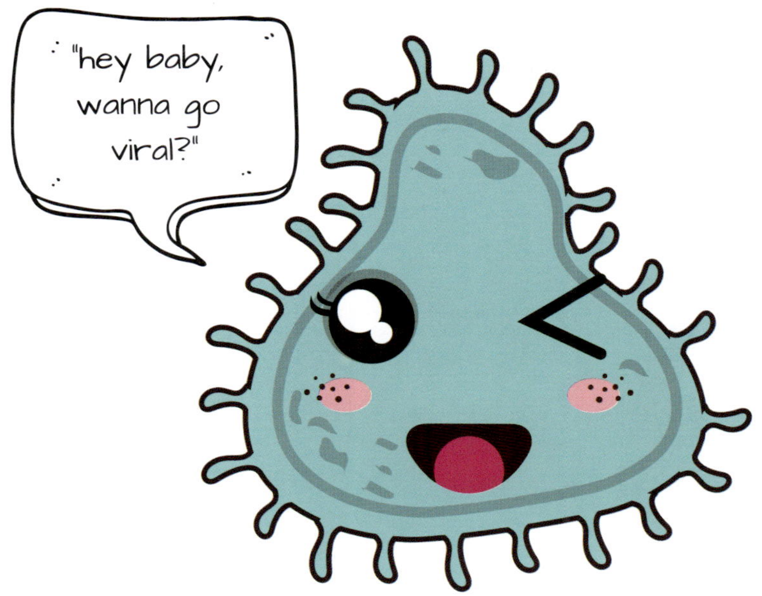

92.

USE VLOGS

CREATE UP-TO 1 MINUTE VIDEO CLIPS WITH KEY TAKEAWAYS ACROSS YOUR TOPICS OF EXPERTISE. ADD THIS TO YOUR SOCIAL PROFILE. THIS GIVES THE SEEKERS AN IDEA OF RANGE AND DEPTH OF TOPICS YOU CAN SPEAK ON.

93.

Audience Fancy One-on-One Connect with the Speakers

Especially once you have spoken, you will find people trying to come up and speak to you. Take time to connect to them, address questions, appreciate the attention. It breaks my heart to see speakers running off from an event the moment their talk is over. This is arrogance at its worst and disrespectful at its best.

94.

IT NEVER HURTS TO GO THAT EXTRA MILE

WHEN PEOPLE WALK UP TO YOU AT A SPEAKER SESSION, MOSTLY THEY CONSIDER YOU TO BE THE END POINT. GO ABOVE AND BEYOND THAT EXPECTATION. WHEN I MET PRAHLAD KAKKAR, INDIA'S AD-GURU, FOR THE FIRST TIME AT AN EVENT, I WAS AMAZED AT THE SPEED AT WHICH HE MADE THE EFFORT TO INTRODUCE ME TO OTHER RELEVANT PEOPLE AROUND US WHO MAY HAVE BENEFITED FROM speakîn AND WHOM speakîn COULD BENEFIT FROM.

HE DIDN'T NEED TO, BUT HE DID GO THAT EXTRA MILE, AND WE ARE STILL TALKING ABOUT IT NEARLY A DECADE LATER.

95.
KEEP UP WITH THE WORLD

BEST SPEAKERS ARE PERPETUALLY UNDER TRAINING. NEW TECHNOLOGY, NEW SKILLS, NEW PROPS, NEW EXAMPLES, FRESH STORIES. ALL OF THAT COMBINED WITH YOUR GROWING EXPERIENCE AS A SPEAKER BUILDS INTO MAKING A STRONGER BRAND AS YOU MOVE ALONG FROM ONE STAGE TO THE NEXT.

96.

TO COMMUNICATE EFFECTIVELY YOU NEED TO UNDERSTAND HOW THE WORLD SEES YOU. THIS IS CRUCIAL WHEN YOU ARE DELIVERING A SPEECH. FOR INSTANCE, YOU MIGHT THINK YOU'RE FUNNY. SO YOU FRAME YOUR NEXT SPEECH WITH HUMOR. BUT WHAT IF NOBODY ELSE THINKS YOU'RE FUNNY? YOU'RE LEFT DELIVERING JOKES FOR 45 MINUTES TO AN AUDIENCE THAT'S DISTRACTED, FIDGETY, AND BORED. IF YOU TAKE THE TIME TO IDENTIFY YOUR UNIQUE DIFFERENCES – THE COMMUNICATION TRAITS THAT YOU NATURALLY USE TO COMMAND ATTENTION – YOUR AUDIENCE WILL BE ENTHRALLED AND YOU WILL BE MORE CONFIDENT AND MEMORABLE.

- SALLY HOGSHEAD

SPEAKER AND INTERNATIONAL AUTHOR

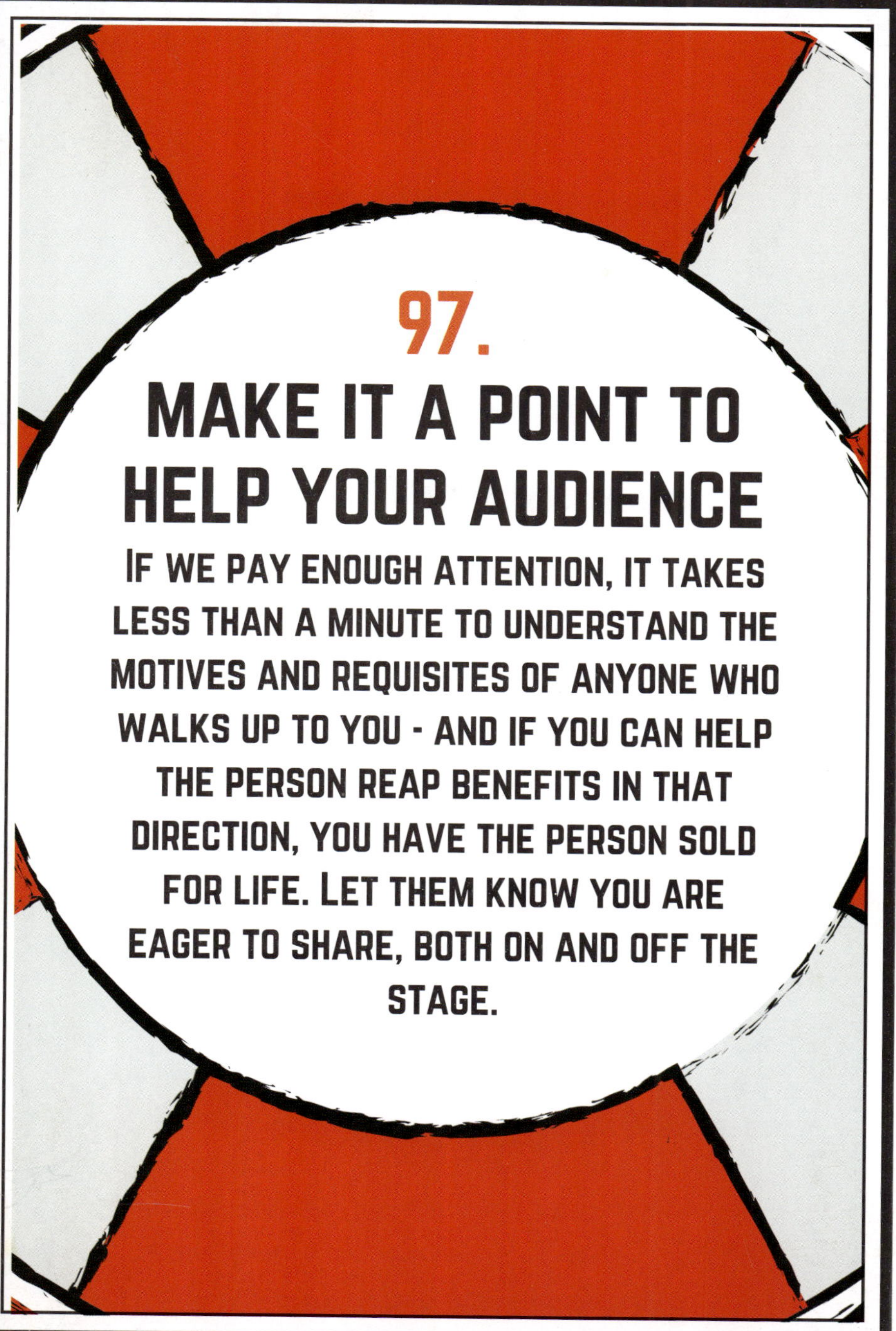

97.

MAKE IT A POINT TO HELP YOUR AUDIENCE

IF WE PAY ENOUGH ATTENTION, IT TAKES LESS THAN A MINUTE TO UNDERSTAND THE MOTIVES AND REQUISITES OF ANYONE WHO WALKS UP TO YOU - AND IF YOU CAN HELP THE PERSON REAP BENEFITS IN THAT DIRECTION, YOU HAVE THE PERSON SOLD FOR LIFE. LET THEM KNOW YOU ARE EAGER TO SHARE, BOTH ON AND OFF THE STAGE.

98.

DO NOT HESITATE TO LOOK AROUND

BEFORE A TALK, SOMETIMES IT HELPS TO WANDER THE ROOM AND MEET A FEW PEOPLE. IT HELPS YOU TO GET A VIBE FOR THE RO24OM. ARE THEY TIRED? ARE THEY EXCITED? ARE THEY EXPERTS ON THIS TOPIC YOU'LL BE COVERING OR ARE THEY COMPLETE NEWBIES?

99.

DO NOT FORGET TO END WITHIN YOUR ALLOTTED TIME

AUDIENCE, ORGANIZERS AND FELLOW SPEAKERS - EVERYBODY HATES IT WHEN A SPEAKER GOES OVER THEIR TIME.
FIVE MINUTES CAN BE THE DIFFERENCE BETWEEN "I WOULD LOVE TO HEAR THEM SPEAK SOME MORE" VS "THEIR TALK FELT A LITTLE TOO LONG."

100.

YOU ARE NOT FINISHED YET

AUDIENCES, ESPECIALLY IN A LARGE GATHERING CAN BE VERY EXPRESSIVE. THIS IS NOT NECESSARILY A BAD THING SINCE MANY A TIMES IT HELPS IN GETTING IMMEDIATE FEEDBACK WHEN OFF-STAGE. MINGLE, SOCIALISE, MAKE THE EFFORT TO CONNECT EVEN AFTER YOU HAVE DELIVERED. THERE WILL BE PEOPLE COMING UP TO YOU TO TAKE A SELFIE - LET THEM HAVE IT. APPRECIATE THE APPRECIATION.

Photo credits: The Atlantic

101.

KEEP GOING - ONE THING LEADS TO ANOTHER

BEING A SPEAKER GIVES YOU A FANTASTIC RECOLLECTION AMONGST AUDIENCE AND FELLOW SPEAKERS. LEVERAGE THESE RELATIONSHIPS. MEET AS MANY PEOPLE AS POSSIBLE, RESPOND TO EMAILS, WRITE BACK TO INTERESTING PEOPLE YOU MET, EXCHANGE CARDS AND THEN STAY IN TOUCH.

REMEMBER BEING A SPEAKER IS ALL ABOUT PEOPLE - ENJOY THE JOURNEY. KEEP speakîn